Copyright © 2021 Kelly and Evelyn Oberheiden
Kind Heart Books, LLC— All rights reserved
www.kindheartseries.com

Book Design and Illustrations by Tasya Nabiella

Published in the United States by RIA JAY Publishing
3355 Lenox Road Suite 750 Atlanta, GA 30326
www.riajay.com

ISBN 978-1-955727-05-1 (Hardback) ISBN 978-1-955727-03-7 (Paperback)
Printed in the United States of America First printing October 2021

We dedicate this magical story of kindness
to the best parents and grandparents.

Steve and Laura Driscoll

The morning breeze tickled Kindheart's nose,
as the sunrise rose.

Butterflies and dragonflies flew all around,
singing good morning with a magical sound.

Smiling and frolicking along,
Kindheart sang her
beautiful song.

Shine, Shine, Shine
Be Kind
Shine your kindness on

When you're kind
You will shine
Shine your kindness on

Enjoying the morning sun,
Kindheart was ready for some fun.

She marveled at the sparkling pond,
that was glistening in the sun.

Colorful lily pads floated nearby.

Then she spotted a turtle that
looked rather shy.

"Hello there," she said to the turtle.

No answer.

"Hi turtle. Are you ok?"

The turtle slowly came out of its shell.

"Hi! Good morning, I'm Kindheart."

The turtle still didn't say anything.

"Are you ok?" Kindheart asked again.

"I'm very shy," the turtle said softly.

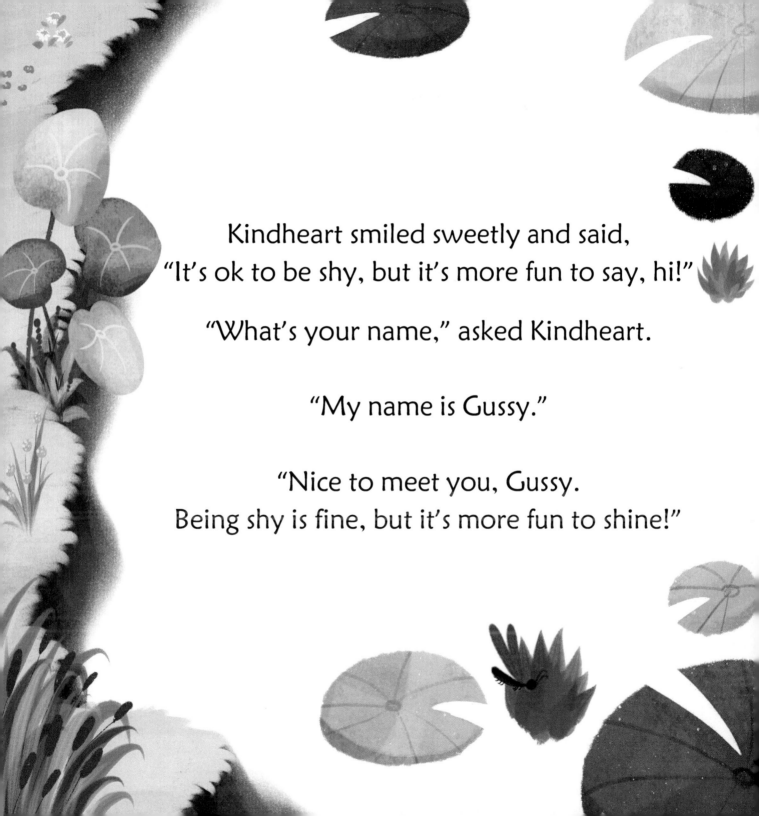

Kindheart smiled sweetly and said,
"It's ok to be shy, but it's more fun to say, hi!"

"What's your name," asked Kindheart.

"My name is Gussy."

"Nice to meet you, Gussy.
Being shy is fine, but it's more fun to shine!"

"What do you mean?" Gussy asked Kindheart.

"Gussy, you can shine your kindness to others by simply saying, 'hi.' Try singing this with me..."

Look them in the eye,
Smile and say, hi!

They sang the song
While smiling and shining along

Look them in the eye,
Smile and say, hi!

"Look there Gussy! There is a fish swimming close by. Try and shine."

Gussy smiled and sang the song.

Look them in the eye,
Smile and say, hi!

"I did it Kindheart! I said, hi.
And I wasn't shy. I can shine!"

"I told you saying 'hi' is more fun than being shy.
And now, Gussy, you're ready to shine!"

They went along singing the song.

Saying 'hi' to all those that came along.

"Thank you for showing me how to shine, Kindheart. Your kindness helped my shyness."

Kindheart smiled and sang her song to Gussy.

Shine, Shine, Shine
Be Kind
Shine your kindness on

When you're kind
You will shine
Shine your kindness on

"I'm so proud of you, Gussy!

Keep shining your kindness to the world!"

Made in United States
North Haven, CT
06 November 2021